Garth

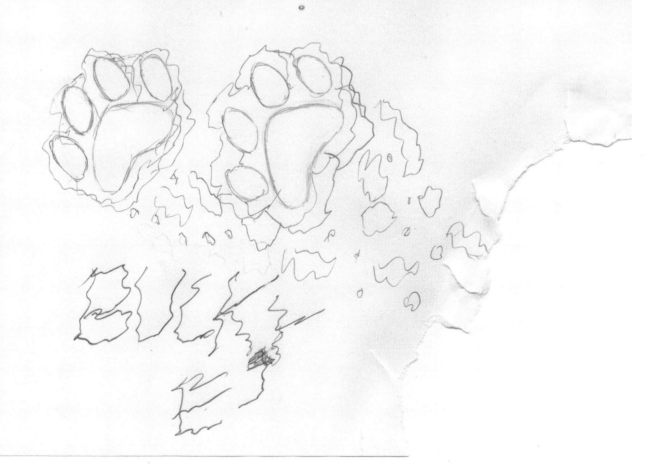

BUKY

Check Out All Of Our Books In The RED BUNDLE-

Volume 1-

"The Mysterious Fence"

Volume 2-

"The Noise From
Under The Bed"

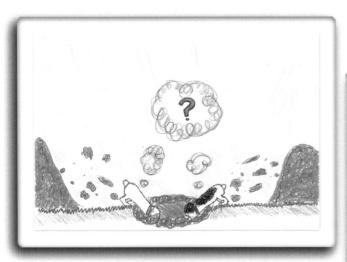

Volume 3-

"The Missing Chew Toy"

Volume 4-

"The Day They Got Picked"

www.buckeyandgarthadventures.com

Buckey & Garth™

Adventures In...

"The Noise From Under The Bed"

Created By:

Dombrowski Family Creations for Children's Growth and Enjoyment, Inc.

Lead Author :   Ken Dombrowski
Assisted By :   Danielle Dombrowski
                  Lauren Dombrowski
                  Michelle Dombrowski

Illustrated By :   Danielle Dombrowski
Assisted By :   Lauren Dombrowski

Published By:

Silver State Family Publishers, LLC

Buckey & Garth ™

Adventures In...

"The Noise From Under The Bed"

ISBN 978-1-4507-3688-6

Buckey and Garth™

-Introduction-

Our family adopted two "Morkie" (Maltese and Yorkie mix) puppies and found so much joy in their personalities that it inspired us to share their adventures with the world.

The two puppies have distinct personalities, Buckey's color is off white and he is a real adventurer, he will climb, jump, or get into, anything and everything he sees, you will find that in the stories he will tend to embellish stories and make things up as he goes along.

Garth, on the other hand, is the black and white pup, and he is the much more cautious one, he tends to follow behind and watch as his brother gets into more and more trouble, but don't be fooled, Garth has a real spunky side to him.

From our family to yours, please enjoy the series of adventures of, **Buckey and Garth**™.

"Buckey!" barked Garth, "what in the name of furry, butt sniffers, are you doin' now?"

"I'm helpin' this carpet," replied Buckey.

"Helping the carpet do what?" asked Garth.

"I'm helpin' it get free, cuz it's stuck to the ground, and I'm gonna pull it up so it can go other places. I really think that Mama and Big Daddy will really like what I'm doing."

"Buckey! What in the world are you doin' to my carpet?" hollered Mama.

"I think you need to scoot, right now!" barked Garth. "Mama does not sound happy about her carpet being pulled up and set free."

"But I heard Mama say that the living room needed to be picked up, so I thought I'd help by pulling up the carpet for her." said Buckey as he scurried into the next room.

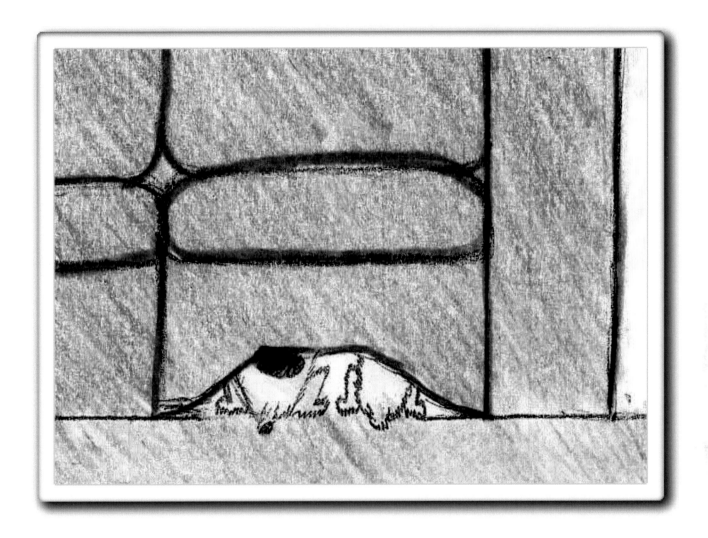

"I think you might be in big trouble this time, Buckey," said Garth. "I'm talking about whimpering, and crying, so you had better turn on the water works type of in trouble, you might not be cute enough to get out of this one."

"Do you think more trouble than the time I tried to wash the pillows by putting them on the lawn for the sprinklers to clean them?" asked Buckey.

"That was pretty bad, too," replied Garth.

Time To Go.....

"I'm gonna head for the backyard," said Buckey.

"What ya gonna do in the backyard?" asked Garth. "I'm pretty sure that they'll look for us back there too!"

"In the backyard I'm gonna defeat that mean, mysterious fence yet once and for all by using my super-stratosfastic double prime maximum overdrive fence melting ray gun." said Buckey.

"Where did you get such a gun? I have never seen it, does it need batteries? Where do you hide it? What color is it? Is it heavy? Did it come with a warranty? Can it also melt cheese?" asked Garth, with curiosity and confusion.

"Well, if I had a gun like that, I would use it on that fence so we could chew on our favorite flowers," said Buckey. "I'll start working on the blueprints right away and should have something drawn up soon." Buckey said convincingly.

Mama grabbed Buckey and Garth, and stuck them in the bedroom so they couldn't get into any more trouble while she cleans up their latest mess.

"Man, that was close. I thought she was really gonna give it to us!" said Buckey.

"Give it to us? Why give it to us, I didn't do anything!" barked Garth.

"Well you know, according to law {711, alpha niner, dash 6DG, paragraph chewy-bone, dot Oh Yah!...} You are just as guilty, because you didn't do anything to stop me." replied Buckey.

"Hold on!" barked Garth. "I heard something under the bed, kinda like scratchin' and hissing."

Buckey replied, "I didn't hear anything. Are you sure?"

"Wait a minute! I heard it too!" barked Buckey.

"Maybe it's a monster, or those bed bugs that Mama's always warning us about," said Garth.

"Well, whatever it is, I think you should go get it Buckey," said Garth.

"Me? Why Me?!" barked Buckey.

"Because it's your fault we got locked in here with a monster, so you should go get it with your super duper stuff-melting ray gun doodad thingy." replied Garth, with confusion and hesitation.

In The Closet.....

"I think we're safe in here from the puppy-eating bed bugs," said Garth.

"Yeah, but, uh, um, I heard about a monster that lives in the closet, called a 'hanger' and it will hang you, if it catches you," said Buckey with a scared low whisper of a bark, so as not to wake the merciless hanger monster of the closet.

AHHHHH!!!.....

The pups go darting out of the closet barking and crying, "Don't get me, you mean closet hanger monster dude!" barked Buckey

"I'm gonna tell Big Daddy on you and he's gonna stake you on a leash in the yard and not give you any treats!" cried Garth.

"We still don't know what's under the bed making those scary noises." said Garth.

"Oh no! There are more noises. It's like a snake doing the hissing sounds or maybe it's a mouse that farted." said Buckey.

I'm Go'in In.....

"I see something!" barked Buckey, "Oh no! It's got pointy ears and fangs and claws like a dragon!"

"Get back up here, it's gonna swallow you and then you'll be dragon poop!" barked Garth, with excitement and concern.

"Okay, you naughty puppies," said Danielle, "you can come out of the room now, just try to stay out of trouble, or Big Daddy will stake you on a leash in the backyard with no treats."

"Man! Get me outta here!" barked Buckey.

Garth cried, "Yeah!   Me too! I Don't wanna be dragon pooohoohoop."

"Man, those guys are too easy," said Sallie the cat. "I didn't know I looked like a dragon!? Next time I'll hide in the closet and be the merciless hanger monster."

The End...

Coloring Contest

To enter our coloring contest is as simple as 1,2,3-

1. Color the beautiful flower, as nice as you can.

2. Have a responsible grown up cut along the dashed line with a pair of scissors and then tri-fold this page to show the mailing block on the front.

3. Then just visit our website for the mailing address, apply some tape to keep it folded and a postage stamp, and mail it to become part of our ongoing contest.

Please visit our website www.buckeyandgarthadventures.com to see if you have won.

Your Return Address Here

Deliver To :
Silver State Family Publishers, LLC
ATTN: Buckey & Garth Coloring Contest

Fold Along This Dotted Line Second

Fold Along This Dotted Line First

Glossary

adopted: verb: to legally take someone's animal/person and raise it as your own

blueprints: noun: a design plan or a drawn business plan

cautious: adjective: to be aware of problems or dangers

charitable: adjective: helping or assisting people in need

circumstances: noun: a specific condition

comprised: verb: to consist of or include

confusion: noun: don't understand; very uncertain

convincingly: adverb: capable of causing someone to believe that something is true

creativity: noun: the use of imagination or originality

curiosity: noun: a strong desire to know something

defeat: verb: win a battle; to overcome or beat

distinct: adjective: recognizably different or out of place

embellish: verb: to make something prettier by adding decorations or details

endeavor: verb: to try hard to do something

entertainment: noun: the activity of being amused or happy

enthusiasm: noun: intense or eager enjoyment

fault: noun: the person who is to blame for a mistake

frisky: adjective: playful and full of energy

guilty: adjective: to be responsible for a specific wrong action

hesitation: noun: to pause before saying or doing something

hollered: verb: to give a loud shout or cry

incentive: noun: to encourage someone to do something

inspired: adjective: to create a creative impulse in an activity

merciless: adjective: when you show no mercy

naughty: adjective: very badly behaved

personalities: noun: the characteristics that form a person's character

scurried: verb: move quickly with short quick steps

series: noun: a number of a specific event or things one after another

spunky: adjective: wild but courageous

stake: noun: strong wooden or medal post with a point at one end, is driven into the ground

tends: verb: regularly behave in a specific way or have a certain characteristic

warning: noun: a statement that indicates a possible danger

warranty: noun: a written guarantee that a company will repair or replace an item

whimpering: verb: to make a series of low sounds that express fear, pain, or discontent

vital: adjective: when it is absolutely needed or very important

Glossary of Imaginary Words

hanger monster: noun: a creative but made up name for a hanger

super-stratosfastic double prime maximum overdrive fence melting ray gun: noun:a creative but made up name for a pretend gun

7-11 alpha niner, dash 6DG, paragragraph chewy-bone, dot Oh Yah!: noun: a creative but made up law

About The Authors

Our family story is not so unusual, we live in the suburbs of Las Vegas, and have always managed to make a good and prosperous living between myself and my wife Michelle. I was always a General Contractor and Michelle always in the Medical industry. Like many Americans, we felt the financial crunch that started in 2007, and that, coupled with my being diagnosed with a debilitating auto immune disease, left me no options but to close our construction business of 20 years, thus, immediately cutting our income by over 50% and we simultaneously noticed medical bills piling up.

In January of 2010, I had to put my heart aside, and succumb to the reality that our beloved fifteen year old, Golden Retriever named "Bosco" needed to be put to sleep. My daily companion now gone, I was left to dwell the house alone, as I mourned his loss. In April of 2010, our family found ourselves craving the presence of a dog in the house, so we found a local breeder and adopted two "Morkie" puppies at the age of 10 weeks old.

Even though, with my illness, I found myself having difficulties keeping up with our new family members, I still was energized and inspired by their spunk and zeal for life, and it, in turn, helped me to feel better about my condition.

Being truly inspired by Buckey and Garth, I felt the need to share this happiness through writing a Children's Book based on mostly real events, then, I wrote another story and engaged the cooperative efforts of our two daughters, Danielle and Lauren. Danielle, age 12 at the time, has always been a great artist so I asked for her to perform the illustrations and our other daughter Lauren, age 10 at the time, was very helpful and creative with the writing, she solely created and wrote the draft for the story "The Day They Got Picked" volume #4. Michelle, has always been the support of all aspects of the books and granted her creativity to keep things moving when we were stuck for progress.

As this fun family project grew to four books and a board game, we found our family closer than ever before, and we can say that we owe it all to two adorable puppies named Buckey and Garth.

From our family to yours, please enjoy!

Ken Dombrowski

Reading Comprehension Tester

Answer these questions to check your Reading Comprehension Skills. For correct answers and more educational tools, visit our website www.buckeyandgarthadventures.com .

Circle the Correct Answer-

1. Why is Buckey pulling up the carpet?
A.He wants to   B.He wants to be helpful   C.He wants to be trouble   D.None of these

2. What color are mommas slippers?
A. Orange   B. Green   C. Pink   D. Purple

3. Where do Buckey and Garth hide out after Buckey gets in trouble?
A. Backyard   B. The kitchen   C. In the bedroom   D. Under the couch

4. What is in the closet that hangs people or things?
A. The hanger monster   B. Hanger dude   C. A Hanger   D. The merciless Hanger monster

5. What does Buckey put on the lawn to wash?
A. Pillows   B. Tennis balls   C. Blankets   D. None of the above

Fill in the Blank-

6. The blue-_____ are for the super-stratosfastic double prime maxium overdrive fence melting ray gun.

7. _____ stuck Buckey and Garth in the bedroom.

8. Buckey's real _____ states that Garth is in just the same amount of trouble.

9. Garth doesn't want to be dragon_____.

10. Next time _____ will be the merciless hanger monster and scare them.

Essay-

11. What was the thing underneath the bed. Why was it there?
_____
_____
_____

12. Summarize about the overall book, be as detailed as possible._____
_____
_____
_____

Buckey & Garth™

-Children's Growth & Enjoyment Guide-

For more information and assistance with-

- Joining our Book Club
- Grant Offerings
- Fun Contests
- Self Publishing
- Scholarships
- Coupon Savings
- Educational Guide
- Tutoring Services
- Buckey & Garth Fun Virtual Games

Go To www.buckeyandgarthadventures.com

Check Out All Of Our Books In The RED BUNDLE-

Volume 1-

"The Mysterious Fence"

Volume 2-

"The Noise From
Under The Bed"

Volume 3-

"The Missing Chew Toy"

Volume 4-

"The Day They Got Picked"

www.buckeyandgarthadventures.com